ARTHUR CHRISTMAS
ELF INVASION

By
ANNIE AUERBACH

STERLING CHILDREN'S BOOKS
New York

STERLING CHILDREN'S BOOKS
New York

An Imprint of Sterling Publishing
387 Park Avenue South
New York, NY 10016

ISBN 978-1-4027-9244-1 (trade paperback)

Distributed in Canada by Sterling Publishing
c/o Canadian Manda Group, 165 Dufferin Street
Toronto, Ontario, Canada M6K 3H6
Distributed in the United Kingdom by GMC Distribution Services
Castle Place, 166 High Street, Lewes, East Sussex, England BN7 1XU
Distributed in Australia by Capricorn Link (Australia) Pty. Ltd.
P.O. Box 704, Windsor, NSW 2756, Australia

For information about custom editions, special sales, and premium
and corporate purchases, please contact Sterling Special Sales at
800-805-5489 or specialsales@sterlingpublishing.com.

Manufactured in Canada
Lot #:
2 4 6 8 10 9 7 5 3 1
09/11

www.sterlingpublishing.com/kids

It was Christmas Eve.

Santa had a big job to do.

It was time to deliver

the presents!

Santa had lots of elves to help him.

Hundreds of elves waited inside the sleigh.

They were ready to zip down

to the houses below.

Down came the elves.

Down came the presents.

It was an elf invasion!

The elves delivered toys to every home.

Some skied down rooftops.

Some used sucker-shoes

to walk down walls.

Elves didn't use chimneys.

They snuck into windows.

They crawled through vents.

They had to go fast!

The elves were ready for anything,

even a noisy parrot!

The Elf Sergeant shot a snack to the parrot.

The bird caught the nut in mid air!

The Delivery Elf scanned a sleeping boy.

The scanner said, "71 Percent Nice."

He stuffed the stocking with toys

and chocolate coins.

Trouble!

Somebody was awake!

The elves climbed around the open door.

They tiptoed to the Christmas tree.

They placed gifts without making

a single sound.

Mission accomplished!

The elves returned to Santa's S-1 sleigh.

They flew to the next city.

Time for another drop!

Steve was Santa's older son.

He watched over Santa and the elves

from Mission Control.

Steve used high-tech computers.

Steve told Santa where to go next.

Santa climbed down the chimney.

Steve watched Santa very closely.

Sometimes, Santa could get into trouble.

Red alert!

Santa slipped on a skateboard.

A little boy woke up!

Santa hid on the floor.

Santa was silent.

The boy went back to sleep.

"MOO!" went one of the gifts.

Would the noise wake the boy?

Steve told the elves exactly what to do.

One elf put earmuffs over the boy's ears.

Another elf scanned the toy.

He needed to find the batteries now!

The elf had to stop the noise!

He cut the wrapping paper.

He removed a battery.

But the toy still made noise!

The elf used a tiny screwdriver.

He took out the rest of the batteries.

"All clear!" he whispered.

Santa and the elves returned to the S-1.

"Merry Christmas, everyone!"

said Santa.

Everyone thought Mission Christmas

was complete.

But it wasn't.

One present had been left behind.

There had been a mistake!

Arthur was Santa's younger son.

"We can't leave a child out of

Christmas!" Arthur said.

But the S-1 needed repairs.

There was one more present to deliver.

Arthur and Grandsanta took out the

reindeer and the old sleigh.

They flew off into the night.

Arthur was going to save Christmas!